COMMUNITY MAGIC

by

PATRICIA CLEVELAND-PECK

Illustrated by Maureen Bradley

HAMISH HAMILTON
LONDON

HAMISH HAMILTON CHILDREN'S BOOKS

Published by the Penguin Group
27 Wrights Lane, London w8 5tz, England
Viking Penguin Inc, 40 West 23rd Street, New York, New York 10010, U.S.A.
Penguin Books Australia Ltd, Ringwood, Victoria, Australia
Penguin Books Canada Ltd, 2801 John Street, Markham, Ontario, Canada l3r 1b4
Penguin Books (NZ) Ltd, 182–190 Wairau Road, Auckland 10, New Zealand

Penguin Books Ltd, Registered Offices: Harmondsworth, Middlesex, England

First published in Great Britain 1984 by
Hamish Hamilton Children's Books

British Library Cataloguing in Publication Data

Cleveland-Peck, Patricia
Community magic.—(Antelope books)
I. Title
823'.914 [J]   PZ7
ISBN 0-241-11249-4

Filmset in Baskerville by
Katerprint Co. Ltd, Oxford.
Printed and bound in Great Britain at the
University Press, Cambridge

Chapter One

"WILLIAM, WILLIAM, come quick!"

William, who was writing up his nature diary in the kitchen, recognised Emma's voice shouting to him over the hedge. He packed his things up quickly and ran outside. Emma was on her bike balancing against the gate post.

"What is it?" he asked.

"I think we've got a Community Wizard job to do. Look." Emma held out a piece of paper and William ran to look at it, nearly tripping over Spot, his dog, in his excitement.

This was just what he enjoyed – doing magic. Since he and Emma had trained under Wizard Entwhistle the

previous summer they had tried very hard to bring happiness and magic to the people of their village wherever possible. Wizard Entwhistle had gone

2

away, promising to come back and continue their training one day and telling them to carry on with their work meanwhile. Usually the jobs were nothing more than finding lost cats or pushing rain clouds over the horizon on someone's wedding day but each time they received a request William felt the same thrill.

"It doesn't say much," said Emma, handing the paper to William.

"Well, often people don't like writing those sort of things down," said William reading the letter to himself. It said,

Dear Community Wizards,

Please could you come to Pippens, the old house on the marshes, where you are needed? Come as soon as you can.

There followed a squiggle which neither of them could read.

"Pippens?" said Emma, "I don't know a house called Pippens do you?"

"No," replied William, "let's ask at the Post Office. Mrs Butler delivers all the letters, so she'll know."

"We can get some chocolate to eat on the way," said Emma. "Hurry up and get your bike, William."

They cycled down towards the Post Office, Spot bounding along the verge beside them.

"It is great the way you've trained him, William," said Emma when Spot stopped automatically and sat down as they reached the junction with the main road. "He even does it without being told!"

William smiled proudly, he enjoyed being with animals more than almost anything else. Quite a few of the Community Wizard jobs had been dealing

with difficult animals and William had gained a very good reputation. Even Emma, who lived on a farm surrounded by cows and sheep and poultry, couldn't make animals do what she wanted in the same way that William could.

Inside the Post Office the usual Saturday crowd was shopping. Mums and Dads who worked all week relied on this time to catch up with all the local gossip. By the door Miss Benson, the Infants teacher and Mrs Walsh, Emma's teacher were deep in conversation. On seeing William and Emma they looked up, all smiles.

"We're just discussing Book Week plans," said Miss Benson. "Everything is going so well, we shall have story-telling every afternoon, a treasure hunt, competitions and a picnic. I think you'll enjoy it."

The children nodded, a whole week of events connected with books and hardly any proper lessons at all.

"We're looking forward to it," said William, as Emma pushed forward to ask the way to Pippens.

Emma came back from the counter. "It's down at the bottom of Shrubs Hill," she said, offering William a piece of chocolate and stuffing some into her own mouth. "Mrs Butler said that if anyone was living there they must have just moved in because as far as she knew it had been empty for years."

"I hope they don't just want us to help them get straight," said William, pushing his bike out and calling Spot to heel. "Too many people mix up Community Wizard's work with Bob-a-Job."

"Without even the bob," said Emma.

8

Community Wizards never accept money from the people they help although they do receive a small payment from the Department of Social Sorcery.

"It will be a lovely bike ride out that way," said Emma. "Come on, let's make a start."

They sped down Shrubbs Hill, the wind in their faces. At the bottom they stopped. It was indeed lovely. The woods on either side of the lane were thick with bluebells and the scent was unbelievably delicious. Beside the road a clear stream flowed over polished stones. Spot splashed about happily, lapping and sniffing.

"I must say I've never noticed any houses down here," said Emma, looking up and down the road. "We'd better try to find it."

This however, did not prove easy. They cycled from the bottom of the hill out to the bare marshes beyond, looking carefully on either side. They cycled back again. They did this three times before sitting down by the stream thoroughly fed up. William got out a packet of crisps.

"Let's eat these and then have one more try," he said. Emma took a handful from William's proferred crisp bag and then clutched his arm.

"Look at that rabbit," she whispered, pointing. William at once signalled Spot to 'stay'.

"That's not a rabbit, Emma," said William softly, "it's a hare." They gazed at the glossy brown hare which stared back at them from the other side of the road.

"It's really beautiful," said Emma, "I wonder if it would come to you William." Spot watched the hare unblinkingly, ears and eyes alert, utterly still.

William took a crisp from his bag and threw it into the road. To his surprise the hare came forward delicately, took the crisp and nibbled it. Then suddenly it moved. Taking a graceful leap into the undergrowth it stopped and watched Emma and William, its nose twitching.

"How funny," said William in a puzzled voice. But just then Emma noticed the overgrown pillar of what must at one time have been the gateway to a big house. Reaching up Emma pushed back a swathe of ivy to reveal, carved into the pillar, the name Pippens. The children squeezed behind the pillar and found themselves in an overgrown drive. No car or cart had passed this way for many years but there was a faint track as though a person or animal used this route. On this track the hare sat waiting for them.

"The bikes!" Although William still looked at the hare with a puzzled frown he was too sensible to forget the bike for

which he had saved up for so long. "We must at least push them off the road."

"Let's hurry then," said Emma, "we don't want to lose this hare."

When they returned, having hidden their bikes behind the pillar, the hare was still waiting, using the time to give his ears a grooming. On seeing them he bounded off down the track. The children followed a few yards behind.

"A hare," said William to himself, "that's something to put in my nature diary."

As it turned out the whole day was worth recording in William's diary, as it was so full of unexpected events. Emma and William followed the hare at an easy pace until the track gave way to a field in which a pretty Jersey cow grazed in the company of a flock of sheep. Nearby stood an old house sur-

rounded by tall trees and beyond it stretched the marsh, primrose and mauve in the sunlight.

"This must be it," said Emma as they approached the house, "it does look empty." They peered in the windows and the only item of furniture they saw in all the silent rooms was one dusty grand piano.

"Let's try round the back," said William, looking around him. The hare seemed to have disappeared. "Ah," he continued as they rounded the corner of the big old stone house, "someone *does* live here."

The back door was open and there were plates laid on a big scrubbed table. There was a chair with a patchwork cushion and a big bunch of flowers in a jug on the dresser. Spot ran in, his tail wagging. William called him

out with the funny feeling that he had been here before, although he knew he hadn't. They shouted but no one came so they crossed the cobbled yard and looked in the old hayloft and stables but nothing was to be seen except dust and cobwebs.

"Over here," said William suddenly, he had noticed a walled garden with a door half ajar. This was the kitchen garden and had been recently tended as there were rows of seedlings coming up. What made William and Emma jump and Spot give a startled yelp was the figure which rose from the back of the garden to greet them. Clad in black, thickly veiled it was quite unlike anything the children had ever seen.

Emma clutched William's arm nervously, "Do you think it's a witch?" she asked in a scared whisper.

Chapter Two

"NO," REPLIED Wizard Entwhistle, removing his veiled hat, "only a friendly Wizard! I am sorry about this garb but I had everything ready for you when the bees began to swarm." He indicated the back wall of the garden where six or seven beehives stood. "It's perfect for them here under the lime trees which provide such delicious honey," he added.

William's heart beat fast with joy. Wizard Entwhistle back at last! They had almost given up hope that he would ever return to continue their training. More real magic! William enjoyed the Cheering Acts and simple spells which make up the routine work of a Community Wizard but he had been longing to start his Part Two course where he could choose his favourite sort of magic to study. Wizard Entwhistle's unforgettable words on passing William into the Company of Mages, "I'd say you have the makings of a Wizard First Class", had often given William comfort when things went wrong. Smiling, William turned to the Wizard and shook his hand warmly. Emma hugged him hard and he put an arm round each of their shoulders and led them back to the house. In the kitchen William realised what had seemed familiar, the Wizard's old furniture from Hare Lane.

"Why didn't you go back to Hare Lane?" asked William. The cottage there was full of pleasant memories.

"Well," said the Wizard with a

sigh, "I have got to lie low for a while. I have been in a bit of danger to tell you the truth." The children looked at him. He did not seem quite as cheerful as before, he seemed somehow smaller and less lively. They were full of questions but the Wizard hushed them, passing round plates of cakes and drinks of lemonade, "I'll tell all in a minute, meanwhile this place will be ideal to start you two on your Part Twos."

"Yipee," screeched Emma, "we thought you'd forgotten us."

"Of course not," said the Wizard, "you've been doing very well." He patted a thick file. Emma saw that it contained a duplicate of all the reports which she and William sent in to Headquarters each time they did a Community Magic task.

"We had a job to find this place," said William, wiping his mouth on the back of his hand.

"Don't I know it," laughed the old man. "If I'd have been here instead of having to come looking for you my bees would have been seen to an hour ago . . . and as for those disgusting crisps, what happened to those with the little blue packets of salt?"

"That hare was you?" asked Emma.

"Don't you remember when William first came, Emma, you did a little shape change to welcome him? Well, I thought a change might do me good too."

"Well, you took me in," said Emma.

"And you William?" asked the Wizard suddenly penetrating.

"I didn't know it was you," said William truthfully, "but it didn't seem quite right as a hare." William laughed, somehow he didn't think a magic hare would count for his nature diary.

". . . so you see I couldn't get back before. A Quest is one of the most important tasks a Wizard can be given." The Wizard poured more lemonade.

"What sort of a Quest was it?" asked William.

"Not a very pleasant one," said the Wizard sadly. "Do you remember when you both started magic I told you that the most important thing is how you use your Power? How all the magic I teach is for Good and how any Mage who uses his Power for selfish or evil ends is in the deepest trouble?"

The children nodded.

"Well," the Wizard sighed, "one such wrongdoer has been detected and when this happens Mages are brought to Council and someone is sent to remove the wrongdoer's Power," he sighed again. "That someone was me but things did not go well. These evil ones are clever, make no mistake. Have you got your tearstones safe?"

The children felt for the holed stones which they always wore round their necks and in which their Power as Mages was stored.

"You remember that I told you that these stones are both amulet and talisman. That means that as well as Power stores they will protect you against evil charms and influences, which may be necessary if you are near me, for the Evil one will try to find me and destroy me if I cannot do so first."

"What happened then?" asked William. "What went wrong?"

27

"At first all was fine," said the Wizard, "I located the wrongdoer easily enough by the power of Scrying. I was worried to see that most of the harm was being done through children. Just as we find that children make the best Community Wizards so the Evil Powers, too, wanted to use children; so I followed wherever the wrongdoer went, trying to undo the evil. All through the land I went from the busiest cities to the most remote corners of this country, up into the land of castles and wide sandy beaches of the north and onto the islands of Callers, Crumstone and Fang . . ." the Wizard's voice sunk low. "There we did battle and the evil one dealt me a bitter blow. I wanted to continue for I could see success so near but the Council of Mages decided to take me off the case

and put a younger Mage in charge. Between ourselves I think they feel that I am past it. I am sure that they have bought this place as a Rest Home for worn out Wizards – not that they said so – but the way they kept talking about pension schemes . . . So for the moment I am to live quietly here and continue with you two. Not," he added looking at their worried faces, "that I am not delighted to do Part Two with you. It's just that a Quest is a Quest and should be finished, not left before the end."

"I am sure that they did it for your own good," said Emma "if you were in danger, I mean."

"Yes, probably," said the Wizard, "but haven't you found that things done for your own good are never as much fun as things done for the sake of themselves? Now, enough of this. Let's

talk of jollier things. Tell me what's been going on in the village and what have you two been doing with yourselves?"

William and Emma brought the Wizard up to date with all the village affairs, telling him how William's mother had won a trip to Spain for two from a cornflakes competition. "I went to stay at Emma's and her Dad let me help with the animals, which was much more fun. And afterwards at least Mum didn't try to make me eat six bowls of cornflakes a day. It's toothpaste now. She's got a cupboardful at home just to get the entry forms!"

They told the Wizard how much they were looking forward to Book Week with all the exciting events. "Miss Benson is really working hard on it," said Emma.

"Ah, Miss Benson, my rival at the horticultural show, I remember." The Wizard gave a slight smile. "I am sorry that I won't be able to enter this year. Never mind, we'll have plenty to keep us busy with your Part Twos."

Wizard Entwhistle arranged that they should come on Saturday mornings until the end of term, then more frequently during the holidays. The lessons would be separate although much of the practical work could be done together. "We'll have some fun," said Wizard Entwhistle with a smile. Both the children vowed that they would do their best to cheer him up after his bad experiences.

Chapter Three

THE WEEK went fast for the children. On the Monday Mr York, the headmaster made final announcements for Book Week. The whole of the following week would be made up of activities connected with books and reading. There was to be an all-day outing to visit a paper mill and a printers, there were to be competitions for the best hand-written book, fiction and non-fiction, and the best collage. There was to be a fancy dress party at which the children were to dress as book characters, there was to be a surprise picnic and every afternoon different people were coming in for story telling sessions. The culmination of the week, however, was to be the visit to the school of a famous children's author Miss Elvimia O'Neeth who, according to Mr York, on hearing of their event had written to him offering to come and talk to the children. Mr York said he had accepted her kind offer and she was coming on Friday. "I confess," he added, "that her books were not previously known to me but," and he showed the children a lavish and colourful book, "she has sent me a copy of one of her books which we can read to prepare for her visit which, from her programme, sounds very exciting."

So, practically no real work was done that week and it sped past very fast. The days were spent preparing competition entries and listening to stories. Every afternoon the school gathered in the hall to listen to one of Miss O'Neeth's stories which were pronounced by Mr York as 'excellent mainstream fairy-tale material'. They were very good indeed and reminded William a bit of some of the old Magic Lore which he and Emma had studied. Anything to do with magic interested William, so keen was he to get back to learning more of it.

As he cycled down Shrubs Hill for his first Part Two magic lesson however a more down to earth thought struck him. He wondered how the Wizard managed for shopping while he was 'lying low'. I could bring him some supplies down

each week if he gave me a list, thought William as he whizzed down the hill, Spot stretched out at a gallop behind him.

Later, when William mentioned the shopping the Wizard smiled.

"You're a good lad, William and thank you for the offer but with my little cow and my garden and my bees I don't want for much. And don't forget there are more shapes than one I can take to go to the village."

William remembering the hare, nodded.

"Shape Changes are part of Part Two work," continued the Wizard, "something you'll enjoy. Look, this is my usual shopping form, if you must know."

The Wizard uttered a soft sighing spell and with a shimmering and blurring which William remembered from long ago, he *became* a little old lady complete with felt hat and shopping basket. William couldn't help giggling and Wizard Entwhistle who, after a

another shimmer, returned to his own shape joined in.

"It has it's funny side, I admit, William. But you must agree that no one would recognise me!"

William stopped laughing and paid attention as the Wizard continued, "Shape Changes can be a very useful defence. Say for example that you were my enemy and I wanted to render you harmless. Well, if I was near enough to touch you –" William heard the sighing spell and felt a tap from the Wizard's hand. Then he experienced a rapid dizzy sensation as the grass rushed to meet him. He put out his hands to steady himself and found that his hands were now two of his four little furry feet. Before him the grass rose like tall trees and his back, why his back was covered with prickles. William was a hedgehog!

Two black boulders in front of him moved, he saw that the boulders had laces in them and realised that they were Wizard Entwhistle's shoes.

"You see," said the Wizard looking down, "now I could pick you up and put you in a box without the slightest trouble."

William felt the Wizard's hand touch him again and with that he went zooming upwards and back into his normal form.

"I didn't feel any different," he said wonderingly.

"Of course not," said the Wizard. "*You* are not changed at all, only your shape. It is only an illusion."

"I'd love to learn to do that," said William.

"You will," replied the Wizard, "but of course you know you must only use these spells when it is really necessary for the Good, not just for fun, don't you?"

"Of course," William nodded.

"Right, then lad," the Wizard smiled, "where's your spell book?"

William put his spell book on the table. He had to copy all spells into this

42

book himself and then learn them by heart for, as he had already found out, no spell works well until the magician can say it fluently.

"The first one we'll do is Shape Change – Other Persons. Learning to change your own shape is a bit more tricky so we'll leave that for the moment. When changing the shape of anyone the hard part is deciding what to change them *into*. Each choice must be sensible and thought out. To slow an

enemy down change him into a snail, to help a friend to escape turn him into a hawk . . . you see what I mean?"

William nodded and began to copy out the words of the spell. When he had finished the Wizard said, "Learn that later on because there is something else I want to ask you now. Each Mage comes to prefer one type of work, we all learn the basics but in the end everyone is good at different things. You've had a good bit of experience in your Community work," he flicked through the file again. "Tell me William, what sort of work do you like best? What would you enjoy learning more about?"

William looked at the Wizard. He had thought about this a lot.

"I like the Herbal side," he said hesitating, "because I enjoy growing things, but most of all . . ." now that the

44

moment had come William felt a bit silly, "most of all I would like to learn, if it is possible, to talk to animals."

Wizard Entwhistle did not look very surprised but just nodded wisely, "A very good choice. For some while now I have thought that you had the whisper . . ."

"The what?" asked William.

"That you are a whisperer. It is a gift, William, like some people are musical and others can draw but it is one that is more secret, like the one which enables some people to find water. A whisperer talks to animals not in words, although words can be important, not by spells but mind to mind. In the old days the services of whisperers were called upon if anyone had an unruly dog or a difficult horse. I have seen a Mage charm a bird from the air onto his hand and I have seen another stop a snake in its tracks, a real snake mind, not an illusion. The gipsy people are well versed in this art William, and the secrets are passed from father to son."

William was thrilled. It was as though the Wizard had given him a lovely, mysterious present.

"Like all talents it improves with practise, so there will be things I can teach you but the gift is within you. It is yours and it comes naturally to you. Come outside and I will show you something interesting."

William followed Wizard Entwhistle into the kitchen garden and over to the beehives. The Wizard gave William the veiled hat.

"These are my friends," said the Wizard moving fearlessly amongst the

46

hives, "and I tell them all my secrets and they do what I wish. Watch." The Wizard whispered something to a knot of bees on his hand and they flew back to the hive and started to dance about outside it. Within a few moments a stream of bees came out and settled in a long line in front of William.

"Now you are their friend, too," said the Wizard, bending down and dismissing the bees.

"Oh there you are," Emma's voice floated across the garden. It was time

for her lesson. William could hardly believe it. Why did the same time in magic lessons fly and in maths lessons drag? The Wizard told him to take his spell book and learn the Shape Change Other People spell while Emma had her instruction. William took the book and sat under the lime trees. He could hear the bees buzzing above him and wondered at the Wizard's power to make them do what he wanted. At first William had been quite scared of the bees. The really intense noise of the buzzing in the hives had surprised him but now he watched them with affection. As William sat, half-learning the spell and half happily day-dreaming about his luck in being a whisperer, he heard thunder roll, saw the sky darken and rain fall. The next moment the house was lost in a thick mist which was followed by

blazing glorious sunshine. William took not a bit of notice. Emma, he knew, had chosen to be a Weatherworker as her special subject.

How to find out more

Chapter Four

BOOK WEEK was proving a great success. Everyone enjoyed seeing the whole school decorated with colourful pictures and posters and the story telling sessions and competitions had made a great change from lessons. Emma had won the fancy dress book character prize by coming as Pippi Longstocking, an untidy sort of girl, which had not needed much effort from Emma. William's nature diary had come second in the non-fiction home-made book competition. (The winner was Rob Turner who knew everything there was to know about CB radios and had written a beautiful 150 page manual on them).

The picnic on the Thursday afternoon had been great fun, too. Everyone had handed in some money and Miss Benson had prepared a 'Wind in the Willows' picnic which they had taken and eaten in the water meadows.

Now the great excitement was the visit of the famous author. No one at Bickers Primary had ever met an author, unless you counted (and most people didn't) the vicar, who had written a slim volume of poetry in his youth.

Mrs Walsh kept assuring the children that authors are "quite ordinary, mothers and fathers doing a job of work, just like the rest of us," but no one quite believed this.

The only slight hitch had been the fact that Mr York had been let down by his suppliers regarding the copies of Miss O'Neeth's book.

"Look at this outrageous inefficiency," he said crossly in the staff room, "the fools returned my order with the comment 'neither author nor publisher known to us,' when," and he held up the book Miss O'Neeth had sent to him, "I quoted all the details including the ISBN number."

So the children would have to wait to buy themselves copies, not that this worried many of them as they sat expectantly in the hall on the Friday afternoon waiting for their first glimpse of the visiting author.

As William remarked later, that seemed to be the last thing most people could remember clearly. They were all aware of the arrival of Miss O'Neeth and took in the fact that she was tall, thin, middle-aged with long dark straight hair and that she had a lovely, melodious voice. She sat at the front of the hall with Mrs Walsh on one side of her and Mr York on the other. The whole school – 53 pupils – sat in a two-deep semi-circle at her feet. Miss Benson sat at the back in case anyone felt sick or had to go out.

Miss O'Neeth had a big basket of papers with her and she began by showing them a small exercise book, not unlike the ones they used at school, in which she started her stories. Then

she brought out a typed script with lots of crossing out which she called her 'first draft', then some funny long printed pages which she said were 'galley proofs' and finally the pages of the book before they were bound together to make a proper book. She talked about her life as a writer and how it gave her the perfect excuse for meeting all sorts of people and asking them the sorts of questions that most people would like to ask but didn't dare. She seemed very friendly and kept stopping and gazing at the children and asking them if they understood and if they had any questions.

It was when Anna Elphick asked if Miss O'Neeth travelled a lot to get materials for her books, that William noticed a funny thing. Miss Benson was sound asleep! William felt very put out.

It seemed so rude. After all Miss O'Neeth was a visitor and to fall asleep in her talk made it seem as though the talk was boring, which it wasn't. William was toying with the idea of telling the person next to him to tell the person next to them, and so on, to give Miss Benson a nudge, when he noticed with real surprise that the person next to him was asleep too. A feeling nearing panic came over William when he looked at Miss O'Neeth and saw that Mrs Walsh and Mr York were asleep as well! In fact, as William looked round the hall desperately, almost no one was awake.

Miss O'Neeth, thank goodness, did not appear to have noticed and continued answering the question although Anna, who had asked it, was snoring gently.

"Yes," William heard her say, "travel is one of the great bonuses. Recently I made a most exciting journey through our lovely northern countryside. The adventures I had amongst the old castles on the wide sandy beaches! Why my next book will almost write itself if I retell what happened on the islands of Callers, Crumstone and Fang . . ."

William, who had been sitting up trying to look very alert to make up for the state of his schoolmates, wondered where he had heard those names before. Was it in geography? Memory had never been William's strong point. Just then he was aware of a movement among the children on the floor. Emma was crawling round the outside of the semi-circle to join him.

"William," she whispered hoarsely,

"we must do something. Don't you see we're the only ones awake, she's bewitched everyone else."

"Betwitched?" William looked at Miss O'Neeth again.

"That's her, silly, the one who is after Wizard Entwhistle. I reckon it is only these that are protecting us." Emma drew her tearstone out from under her collar. As she did Miss O'Neeth gave a furious cry.

"Who is that? Which of you is the cunning-man's minion? I smell you, stand up."

"Quick William, what shall we do?" Emma looked pale. William racked his brains. Then he had an idea. "Render an enemy harmless," yes, he knew this one, it was the last thing he had learnt and it was fresh in his memory. Nothing could go wrong and it would give them time to ask Wizard Entwhistle's advice.

William darted to the front of the hall as fast as he could and stood before Miss O'Neeth who thought he had come to own up to having the tearstone. Quickly he whispered the soft sighing spell without either getting it wrong or forgetting it. Everything would have been perfectly all right had not Mr York slithered forwards in his chair and, stopping mid-snore, jerked his arm

forward, touching for an instant William's outstretched hand. Miss O'Neeth jumped up with a delighted cry. For some reason the word 'hag' came into William's mind although it was a word he had never used before. She ran out of the hall crackling with terrible laughter, pausing only to point her long red fingernail before disappearing.

William followed the direction of her pointing finger and, with a horrified and sickened glance, saw that Mr York, headmaster of Bickers Primary school, had received the full force of the shape change spell. Mr York was now a snail.

"Don't for goodness sake tread on him," said Emma anxiously. "Do you know how to get him back?"

The snail, a small, delicate, rather pretty little thing was attempting to

descend the leg of the chair, his feelers waving daintily.

William's mind was whirling. He had been surprised to have remembered the spell so well and was pleased with his choice of a snail as a Change Object. Could he remember the next bit?

"What if she comes back?" asked

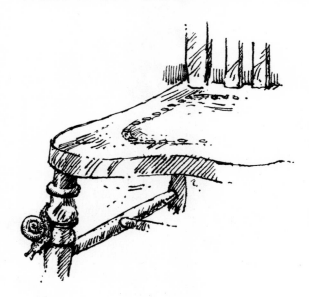

William. They both looked towards the door. "She won't," said Emma, "she'll be after Wizard Entwhistle now that she knows he's somewhere near. Quick William turn Mr York back."

They glanced towards the chair, then back towards each other, their faces dismayed. The snail had gone.

Chapter Five

ONE OF the most surprising things, William remembered later, is the amount of ground a snail can cover if it sets its mind to it. This particular snail (neither of them could bring themselves to calling it Mr York) had almost reached the headmaster's office when the children caught up with it.

"You pick it up," said William. Emma gave him a disgusted look. "It's only fair," continued William hurriedly, "I've got the spell to say."

"I hope he doesn't remember this bit," said Emma grimly as she put the small but slimy creature carefully into her hand. Moving as quickly as she

68

could she returned the snail to the seat
in the hall. William stood over it and
tapped it lightly saying the words of
Restoration to Original Shape.

As Mr York woke with a start he
began clapping automatically, as if he
was quite used to sleeping through

lectures. This seemed to wake everyone else and they, too, joined in the applause. Such was the bewitchment however, that although it was obvious that Miss O'Neeth had left the hall, no one thought this odd and many said that it was the best talk they had ever heard. No one, funnily enough, remembered much about the content.

By now it was almost home-time and William and Emma headed for the door to be first out.

Spot was waiting outside in his usual place for William.

"Go and get your bike," said Emma. "Meet me at the Post Office in ten minutes. We may still have time to warn Wizard Entwhistle that she is here."

They rushed red-faced into the kitchen at Pippens, praying that they were not too late.

"Oh thank goodness," said Emma, collapsing into a chair when she saw the Wizard blithely reading a copy of The Beekeeper's Weekly. Quickly they told him what had happened. Instead of appearing worried the Wizard looked positively delighted at the news.

"So there is hope," he said, "hope that I may succeed in my Quest."

"What about the danger?" asked Emma. "She did look a strong sort of character."

"She is, but I know quite a few of her wily ways by now. Come, let's see what she is up to. We'll feel better if we know exactly where she is."

The Wizard took them to the water-but at the corner of the house. "I can scry here," he said. William and Emma looked puzzled.

"Some use a crystal ball, some a mirror but I can see as well in any pool

or even sometimes in my own finger nail. Look into the water now."

The Wizard murmered some spell words and suddenly a picture appeared on the calm surface of the water.

"I see her," said Emma. "Look she is near the gateway in Shrubs Lane."

William could see as clearly as a picture on a television screen – black and white but maybe that was the colour of the water – Miss O'Neeth looking at the name Pippens just as they had done on their first visit.

"Good," said Wizard Entwhistle who looked more cheerful than the children had seen him for some time. "We've got time. It is her tearstone we are after, but she must give it up herself. This is what we'll do. I have friends who will help me, you leave Spot here and come with me William. Emma you use

73

Weatherwork to delay and confuse her."

William followed Wizard Entwhistle through the gate of the kitchen garden and towards the beehives. The Wizard bent over the hives, telling the bees what had happened. Within a few seconds the bees streamed out of the hive in a long black line. Wizard Entwhistle smiled happily. "Bees have been connected with magic from the earliest days and being a beemaster has

brought me a lot of pleasure, and help."

He turned back towards the house and William followed calling Spot to heel.

Miss O'Neeth approached the house stealthily, little suspecting they knew she was coming. She tiptoed to the windows and looked in, just as the

75

children had done and then, like them, she came creeping round the corner.

Spot gave a low growl and William told him without words to hush. At once he was quiet.

At that moment one of Emma's mists arose and swirled around Miss O'Neeth confusing her for a moment. Only for a moment though, for she was powerful in magic and soon uttered a spell to clear her way. She was not expecting the next development however, nor could she control it. So when she noticed the thick band of bees making directly for her she took to her heels, running across the drive and jumping the fence into the field. She tried spell after spell without success. Wizard Entwhistle blocked them all. Anger and frustration made forked lightning fly from her feet as she ran, and the sheep

and Wizard Entwhistle's little cow fled from her in terror. On she plunged, driving the animals before her out onto the marshes beyond. Wizard Entwhistle and the children ran after her and the Wizard had almost caught up with her when the bees found their mark and covered her head and shoulders with a living, crawling black mantle.

"At last Elvimia O'Neeth," he chuckled, "and a fair old dance you've led me. Now these bees are real – no illusion – and none of your spells will be of the slightest use. The bees however, will not sting you unless I tell them to and I hope that I won't have to for, as you know, if a bee stings it dies and I would not wish my friends to have to die. However ..."

"Get them off me," she interrupted, moaning. "Just get them off me."

"I'll get them off just as soon as you give me the stone which hangs about your neck."

Her hand flew to her tearstone, "Never!" she cried. But, as a number of bees began to wriggle down the neck of her blouse, she started to whimper.

"Be reasonable," said the Wizard gently, "you are lucky that I am prepared to rescue you from this wretched life. Give me your tearstone and go back to the world as an ordinary person, having learnt your lesson."

She gave a low, howling moan. "You know I could destroy you if I chose," said Wizard Entwhistle becoming more firm, "but for the last time I am offering you peace."

Trembling, the witch loosened her tearstone. As soon as she handed it to the Wizard she changed. Her face bore a puzzled look as though she had woken from a bad dream and without a word she got up and walked across the field and out of their lives.

"That's that, then," said the Wizard brushing down his clothes and giving Emma a satisfied smile. "Now all that remains is to send this tearstone back to Headquarters for fumigation."

It was then that they heard the faint cry.

"What's that?" asked Emma, "has she come back?"

"Over here, help!"

They ran towards the sound and found William balanced precariously on the edge of the dyke which cut the marsh in two.

"I managed to stop the sheep," said William, pointing to where a bunch of sheep grazed nearby, "but your little

cow was so frightened of Miss O'Neeth that she plunged straight in before I could get to her."

They saw the little Jersey cow sunk deep into the water.

"I've stuck a plank under her front legs," said William "but it won't hold for much longer." The cow's frightened eyes never left William's face.

"Good lad," said the Wizard. "You are calming her, that's the most important thing. We'll save her if she doesn't struggle."

"Yes, we must get a tractor and a rope," said Emma who knew about such things. "I heard one over there. Hold on William." Emma sped across the marsh as fast as she could.

William whispered words of comfort to the cow who kept perfectly still and quiet. He kept this up throughout the long moments until the farmer came and put a rope around her front legs and then, taking a shovel, broke down the banks of the dyke so that she would not hurt her legs being dragged out.

Back on the land once more the cow shook herself and began to graze.

"Well I never," said the farmer, "last time something like that happened to one of my cows she was so shocked she couldn't stand up for three days. I don't know how you did it but you can be mighty proud of saving that fine cow, and the sheep too, by the sound of it. What caused the rumpus do you think? We saw the lightning strike and strike again. Some freak storm I suppose? Anyway you give me your name and address my boy, and I'll send something round by way of reward. Yes, its only fair, not many youngsters would have done what you've done."

Later that evening Wizard Entwhistle, Emma and William sat down to a celebration meal. Roast chicken with all the trimmings, honey-sponge trifle and then some of Wizard Entwhistle's special magic sweetmeats, delicious

cake-like sweets which never make you feel full up.

"Now we can really get on with your lessons," said the Wizard. His face was beaming and he seemed his old cheerful self again. "What a cheek that witch had got coming here and making no secret of who she was either."

"How do you mean?" asked William. "We thought she was a famous author."

"Famous author!" snorted the Wizard, he took a pen and wrote out in capitals ELVIMIA O'NEETH, "who ever heard of anyone called that?"

"I did think it might be a pen name," said Emma. The Wizard then took a pair of scissors and cut each letter out.

"You just play around with this for a minute. As anagrams go it is very simple. Five words with one, two, three, four and three letters in each."

Emma solved it quite quickly, "It tells us exactly who she is too," she commented. "I found that an easy anagram to solve."

(I am the evil one)